The Little Rocket's Holiday

Written by Grace Griffiss-Williams
Illustrated by Georgia Lisk

DEDICATION

To my amazing friends

The Little Rocket was hanging out in her back garden, when there was a knock at the door.

She went to answer it and there was Felicity the Dalek.

The Little Rocket had invited Felicity over for a party, but Felicity was very early so she invited her in and they talked for a while in the garden while they waited for the other guests.

"You need a holiday" said Felicity the Dalek.

"You are right!" exclaimed the Little Rocket

Suddenly…….“BOO!” shouted Ashley the Dinosaur and Jude the Giant Ladybird!

"....And what are you doing?" shouted the Little Rocket!

"Well... we... we...." stammered Ashley "...Came for the party", interrupted Jude the Giant Ladybird.

"OK… well we had better have the party out in the garden because you are 52 foot tall!"

"Did we hear you say HOLIDAY?" said Ashley the Dinosaur. "Yes! Yes, you did! I think I *will* go on a holiday!"

After the party the Little Rocket packed her things and got on a bus to the airport and waited for the aeroplane but she was very scared because it was her first time flying.

She was also very, very excited, thinking about what wonders could await her in Istanbul!

The aeroplane was amazing! The Little Rocket sat next to Batman Neddie and Kendra the Deer!I

They talked about
what hotel they were
all staying in.

"Hi." Kendra the Deer
said.
"Hi, where are you
going to?" said the
Little Rocket

"Grey Turtle Lane Hotel" replied Kendra the Deer.

"What about you, Batman Neddie?" asked the Little Rocket.

"The same place", Batman Neddie said.

After the Little Rocket, Batman Neddie and Kendra the Deer went through the security checks and got their bags, they shared a taxi to Grey Turtle Lane Hotel.

It was almost midnight when the Little Rocket, Kendra the Deer, and Batman Neddie got to the hotel, so the first thing they did was set up the room and then go to bed.

In the morning they tried some new breakfast! After breakfast they packed the things back up and got another taxi to the real Hotel.

The first one was only the airport hotel, so they didn't get much sleep because
they heard so many aeroplanes coming in to land, and flying off.

When the taxi arrived, they put their stuff in the boot and they got in.

When they got to the real hotel, they discovered they were all staying on the same level, so they knocked on each other's doors and went out for dinner together.

When they got back, they went straight to bed!

In the morning they went out for pancakes.

Afterwards, they went shopping and then went on a ferry across to the other side of the river, where they found loads of shops and restaurants.

They did a bit more shopping, had lunch and then they went home. By the time they got home it was time for dinner.

"Little Rocket!" Kendra the Deer shouted, the next day, as she pounded on the Little Rocket door.
"It's time to go" shouted
Batman Neddie

"You'll have to go without me", said the Little Rocket. "I'm in the shower."

"OK we will wait 10 minutes for you."

After breakfast, they went to do more shopping, then they went on a tram to some Mosques.

The Little Rocket's favourite one was the Hagia Sophia, but Batman Neddie's favourite was the Blue Mosque, and so was Kendra the Deer's.

The next day, the Little Rocket got a postcard. It was from her friends, back home.

Dear Little Rocket,
We miss you very very much, so we have come to visit, and stay on holiday with you until you come back.
 Much love from your friends,
Jude the Giant Ladybird, Felicity the Dalek, Ashley Dinosaur and Cory the Minion.

The next day, the Little Rocket found that she had flowers by her door!

They were from her friends, and guess what? They were staying next door!

As soon as she had put them in a vase, she went to knock on their door, then they all went out for breakfast.

After that, they all went shopping. Jude the Giant Ladybird bought a Genie in a lamp, and Ashley the Dinosaur loved Harry Potter, so the Little Rocket bought him a Harry Potter scarf.

Felicity the Dalek got a Harry Potter lamp, Batman Neddie got a new Batman figure and Kendra the Deer got some new food that she really liked.

The Little Rocket got postcards for everyone to help them remember Istanbul.

By the time the holiday was over, everyone came back laughing and having fun because they had decided they were going to Splashdown after Christmas…..

but that was *after*
Christmas and after
the Little Rocket's and
Jude the Giant
Ladybird's birthdays!

TO BE CONTINUED!

About the Author:

This book was written by Grace, who is very nearly ten years old. Grace lives in Bournemouth with their mum, dad, and two siblings. Grace is very interested in Harry Potter, Dr Who, and Space. Grace would like to be a Mission Controller but might still find time to write books.

17087016R00032

Printed in Great Britain
by Amazon